Original cartoon strip published in 1999 by DC Comics
(a division of Warner Bros.), 1700 Broadway, New York, NY 10019, USA
This edition published in 2000 by BBC Worldwide Ltd
Woodlands, 80 Wood Lane, London, W12 0TT
Text, design and illustrations © 1999 Warner Bros.
4000 Warner Boulevard, Burbank
California 91522-1704, USA

Printed and bound in Italy by L.E.G.O. Vicenza

ISBN 0 563 47581 1
BBCB 0018

It's a Wonderful Prehistoric Life

It's a Wonderful Prehistoric Life

EVERYONE WAS FEELING THE SPIRIT THIS YEAR, INCLUDING ONE *FREDERICK J FLINTSTONE.*

OFFICE

WE'RE QUITTING EARLY TODAY...

...MERRY CHRISTMAS!

EMPLOYEE MAILBOXES

..MERRY CHRISTMAS!

MR SLATE SURE WAS GENEROUS THIS YEAR... LOOK AT THESE BONUSES!

WOW!

11

16

37

THE END